WarCraft

A is for Azeroth

The ABC's of Warcraft

WARCRAFT

A is for Azeroth

The ABC's of Warcraft

Written by **CHRISTIE GOLDEN**
Illustrations by **SARA VALENTINO**

INSIGHT
EDITIONS

SAN RAFAEL · LOS ANGELES · LONDON

A is for Azeroth,

a magical world that many heroes call home!
Some of these heroes fight for the
Alliance, wearing **armor**.
Here they come now!

B is for the Barrens,
a land of many creatures big and small.

C is for the Children of Cenarius,

some of the **creatures** who live in Azeroth!

Among them are the quiet and gentle dryads, and the wise Keepers of the Grove. The mighty **centaur** are descended from the son of **Cenarius**.

D is for Dwarves,

a strong and sturdy people who live in the mountains and underground; **dragons**, some of whom fight to protect all life on Azeroth; and **draenei**, who came from another world, seeking peace.

E is for Eastern Kingdoms,

where many dwarves, dragons, and draenei live, but also the quel'dorei **elves** in their beautiful forest called **Eversong Woods**.

F is for Festivals and Faires!

The citizens of Azeroth love these fun events, like the Midsummer **Fire Festival** and the Darkmoon **Faire**!

G is for Gnomes,

a race of small people with big brains and big hearts. **G** is also for **gryphons,** as well as **goblins,** who love science—and building things. Though sometimes their machines break down!

H is for the Horde,

who fight for the future of Azeroth, just like the Alliance. Some Horde members are **hunters**. **H** is also for **hero** . . . and you can be one too!

I is for Island,

a small piece of land surrounded by water. This is also called an **isle**. Echo Isles is the home of the Darkspear trolls, who are part of the Horde.

J is for Jungle,

and Azeroth has many of them. Stranglethorn Vale is a large **jungle** in the Eastern Kingdoms. Here you can find trolls, tigers, and waterfalls! Un'Goro Crater has a volcano and dinosaurs—the biggest dinosaur here is called a Devilsaur!

K is for Kalimdor,

home to the Horde races of orc, tauren, and troll, as well as to Alliance races like the **kaldorei,** otherwise known as night elves. Their moonwells are magical pools of light and water.

L is for Light!

The **Light** is a great power of goodness. Priests and paladins use the Light to heal and protect, but the Light can fight an enemy as well.

Libram also starts with **L**. Its pages contain spells that grant the Light's blessing to paladins. The Light's powers are holy magic.

M is for Magic!

There are many different types of **magic** in Azeroth. People use magic to heal, to grow stronger, to shoot bolts of energy, and to turn into animals! Even the finny creatures known as **murlocs** can use a little bit of magic!

N is for Night Elves,

who are very tall and live close to nature. They are the oldest kind of elf in the world, and all other elves are descended from them.

The **naaru** may look like stars, but they are actually beings of pure Light turned into something beautiful!

O is for Orcs,

who founded the Horde. **Orcs** are strong and honorable. They like to ride wolves! Large numbers of orcs live in **Orgrimmar**, the capital city of the Horde that is named after an orc called **Orgrim**.

P is for Pandaria,

where the **pandaren** live. They sometimes explore Azeroth from the back of a giant turtle. They also ride in hot-air balloons!

P also stands for **potions**, which are magical drinks that grant special **powers**, like growing as tall as a giant!

Q is for Quel'Thalas,

the kingdom of the **quel'dorei**. The elves have keen eyesight, which makes them excellent hunters.

Q is for **quest**, too. A quest is a search for something. In Azeroth, people go on many, *many* quests!

R is for Rogue.

A **rogue** can become invisible and step from shadow to shadow! Rogues are often sent to gather important information in secret.

Rangers also move quietly and go unnoticed. That makes it easier to hunt!

S is for Shaman,

who work with the elemental **spirits**. Shaman are powerful enough to cause earthquakes, thunder and lightning, and even floods!

T is for Tauren,

a calm, proud people who respect nature and sometimes fight fiercely to protect it. They are members of the Horde, and their capital city, **Thunder Bluff,** also starts with **T!**

U is for Undead.

The **undead** are people in Azeroth who are alive, but also not. Some undead, who call themselves "The Forsaken," make their home beneath an abandoned castle. They call it the **Undercity**!

V is for Vulpera.

They are people who are foxes. **Vulpera** are small, smart, and a little bit sly. They wander to and fro in their alpaca-drawn caravans, never happy being in one place for too long.

W is for Worgen.

Worgen are people who can turn into **wolves**! They often like to dress in an old-fashioned way. Look at that top hat!

X is for Xuen,

the White Tiger. As one of the four August Celestials, he teaches people when to fight, and when not to fight.

Chi-Ji, the Red Crane, teaches the importance of hope: how to find it, and how to keep it.

Y is for Yu'lon,

the Jade Serpent, who stands for wisdom and faith. She sometimes disguises herself as a pandaren girl named Fei.

Niuzao, the Black Ox, protects the weak and helps people find courage.

Z is for Zandalar,

the birthplace of the entire troll civilization. Thousands of years ago, the **Zandalari** trolls ruled an empire spread all over Azeroth. The beautiful golden temple city of **Zuldazar** is the jewel of **Zandalar**.

Thank you for exploring **Azeroth** from **A to Z**. Farewell, friend!

INSIGHT
EDITIONS

PO Box 3088
San Rafael, CA 94912
www.insighteditions.com

 Find us on Facebook: www.facebook.com/InsightEditions
 Follow us on Twitter: @insighteditions
 Follow us on Instagram: @insighteditions

ISBN: 979-8-88663-020-6

Publisher: Raoul Goff
VP, Co-Publisher: Vanessa Lopez
VP, Creative: Chrissy Kwasnik
VP, Manufacturing: Alix Nicholaeff
VP, Group Managing Editor: Vicki Jaeger
Publishing Director: Jamie Thompson
Art Director: Stuart Smith
Senior Editor: Justin Eisinger
Editorial Assistant: Sami Alvarado
Managing Editor: Maria Spano
Senior Production Editor: Michael Hylton
Senior Production Manager: Greg Steffen
Senior Production Manager, Subsidiary Rights: Lina s Palma

Blizzard Entertainment, Inc.
Licensing: Byron Parnell, Derek Rosenberg
Editorial: Chloe Fraboni, Eric Geron
Art & Design: Corey Peterschmidt
Production: Ed Fox, Brianne Messina, Jamie Ortiz, Amber Thibodeau
Lore Consultation: Courtney Chavez, Damien Jahrsdoerfer
Game Team Consultation: Ely Cannon, Steve Danuser, Korey Regan, Chris Robinson

ROOTS of PEACE   REPLANTED PAPER

Insight Editions, in association with Roots of Peace, will plant two trees for each tree used in the manufacturing of this book. Roots of Peace is an internationally renowned humanitarian organization dedicated to eradicating land mines worldwide and converting war-torn lands into productive farms and wildlife habitats. Roots of Peace will plant two million fruit and nut trees in Afghanistan and provide farmers there with the skills and support necessary for sustainable land use.

Manufactured in China by Insight Editions

10 9 8 7 6 5 4 3 2 1